THE AMAZING SPIDER-MAN

Clash with the Rhino

HarperCollins®, ®, and HarperFestival®
are trademarks of HarperCollins Publishers.

Library of Congress catalog card number: 2008937123
ISBN 978-0-06-162611-1

Book design by Joe Merkel
09 10 11 12 13 UG 10 9 8 7 6 5 4 3 2 1
❖
First Edition

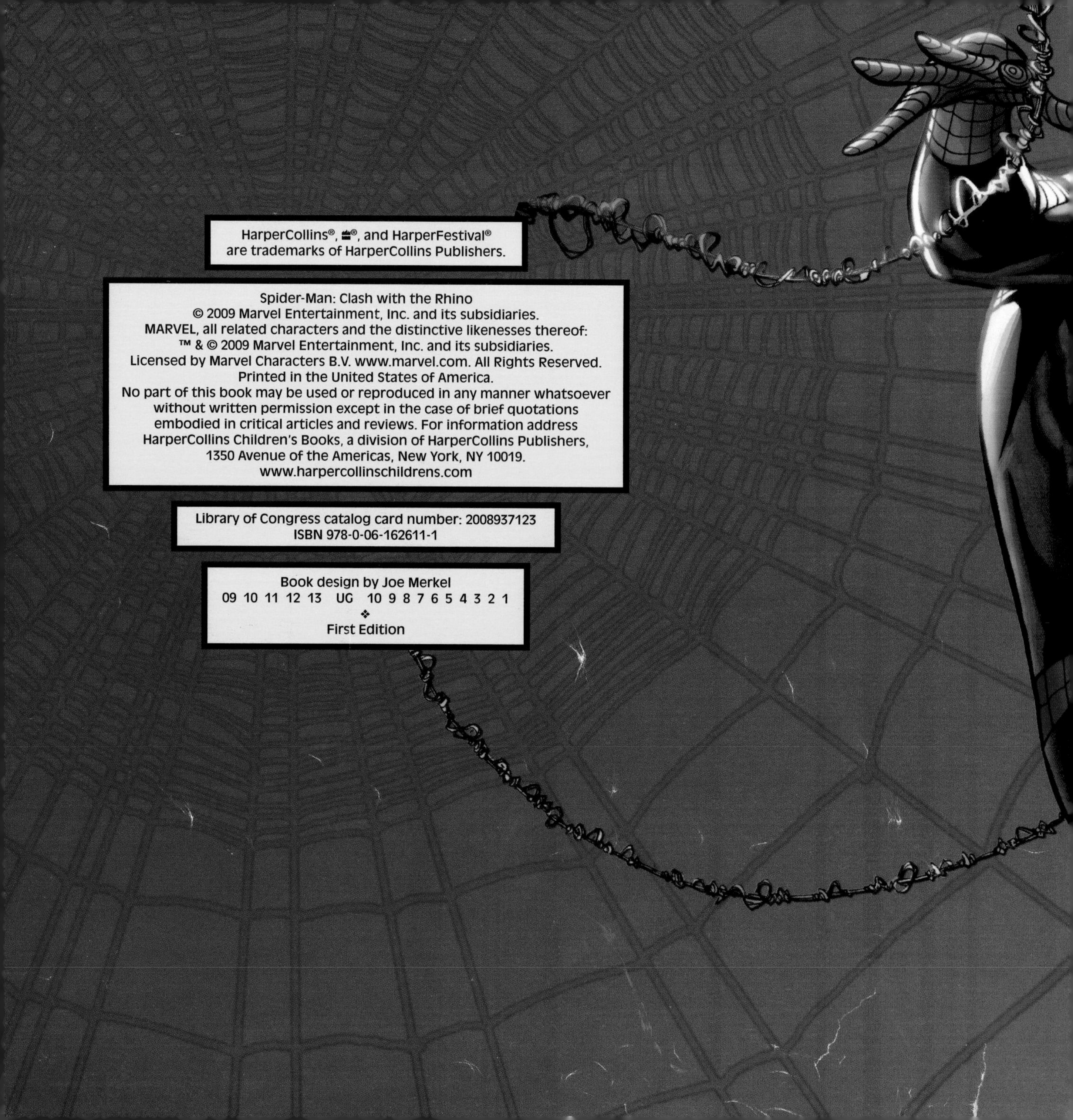

THE AMAZING SPIDER-MAN®

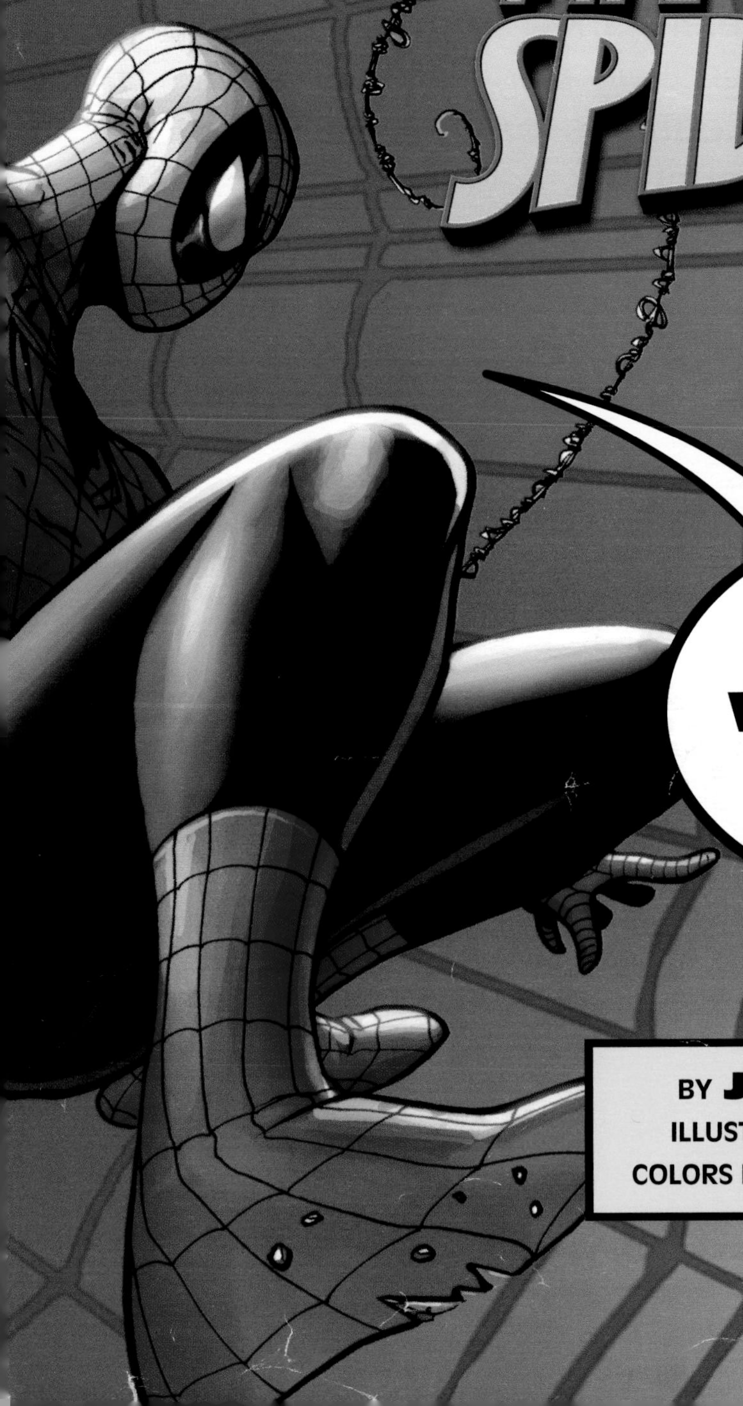

CLASH WITH THE RHINO

BY **Jennifer Christie**
ILLUSTRATED BY **Andie Tong**
COLORS BY **Jeremy Roberts**

HarperFestival®
A Division of HarperCollinsPublishers

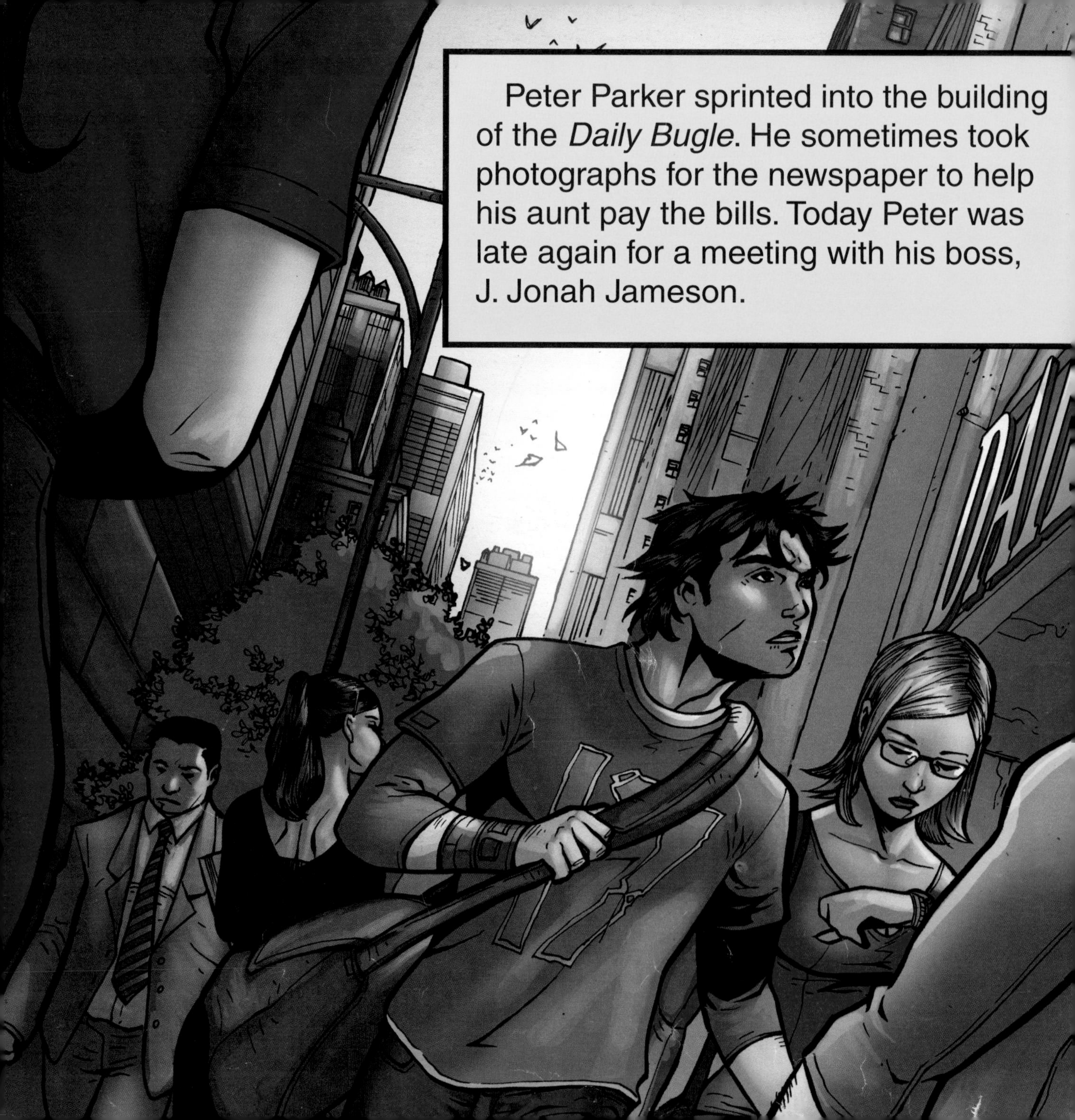

Peter Parker sprinted into the building of the *Daily Bugle*. He sometimes took photographs for the newspaper to help his aunt pay the bills. Today Peter was late again for a meeting with his boss, J. Jonah Jameson.

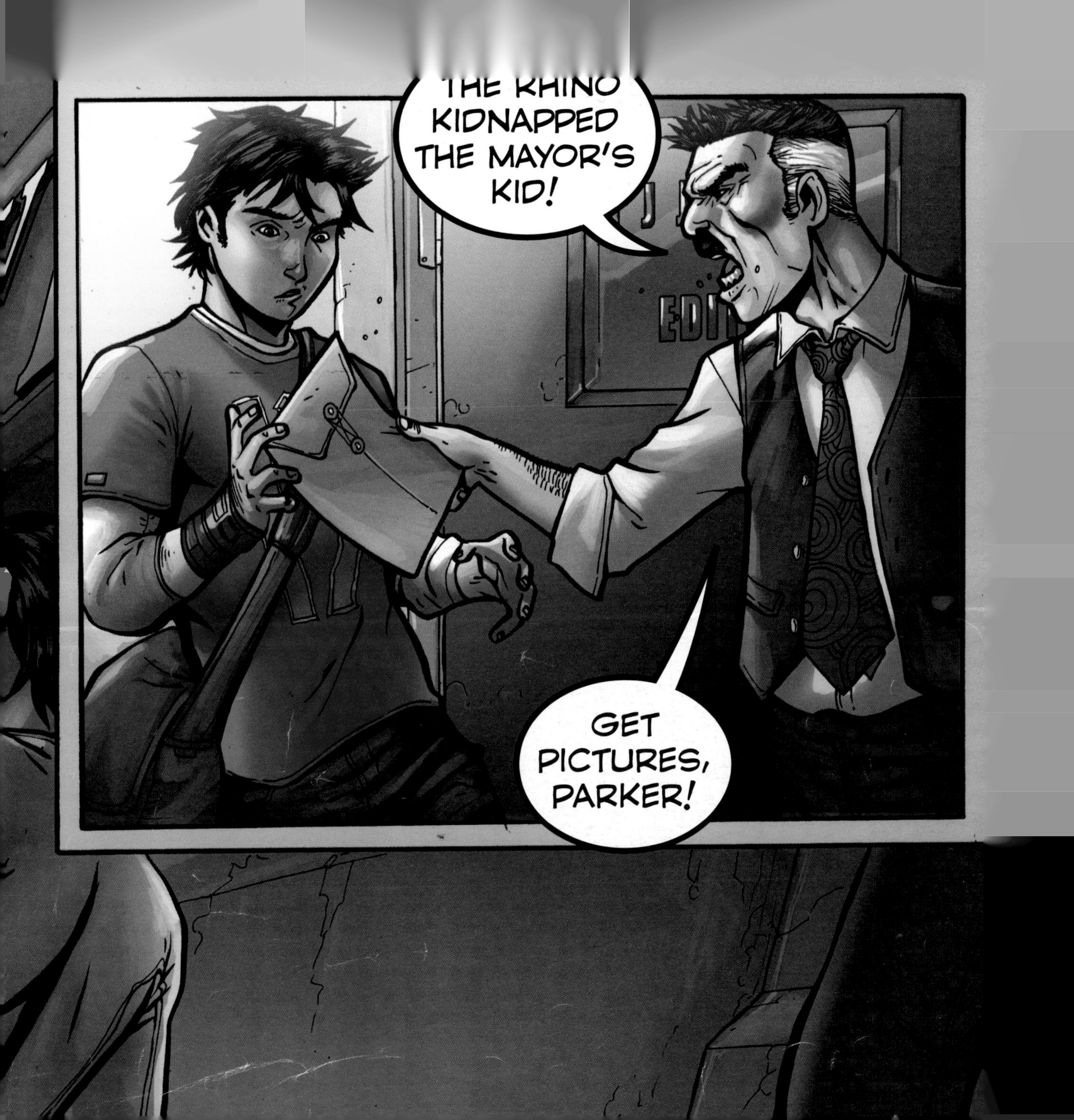
THE RHINO KIDNAPPED THE MAYOR'S KID!
GET PICTURES, PARKER!

The Rhino had razor-sharp horns and superhuman strength. He also wore a special bodysuit made of tough rhinoceros hide.

The Rhino worked for a team of greedy mobsters. After the kidnapping, he left a message from his bosses: PAY UP IF YOU WANT THE KID BACK.

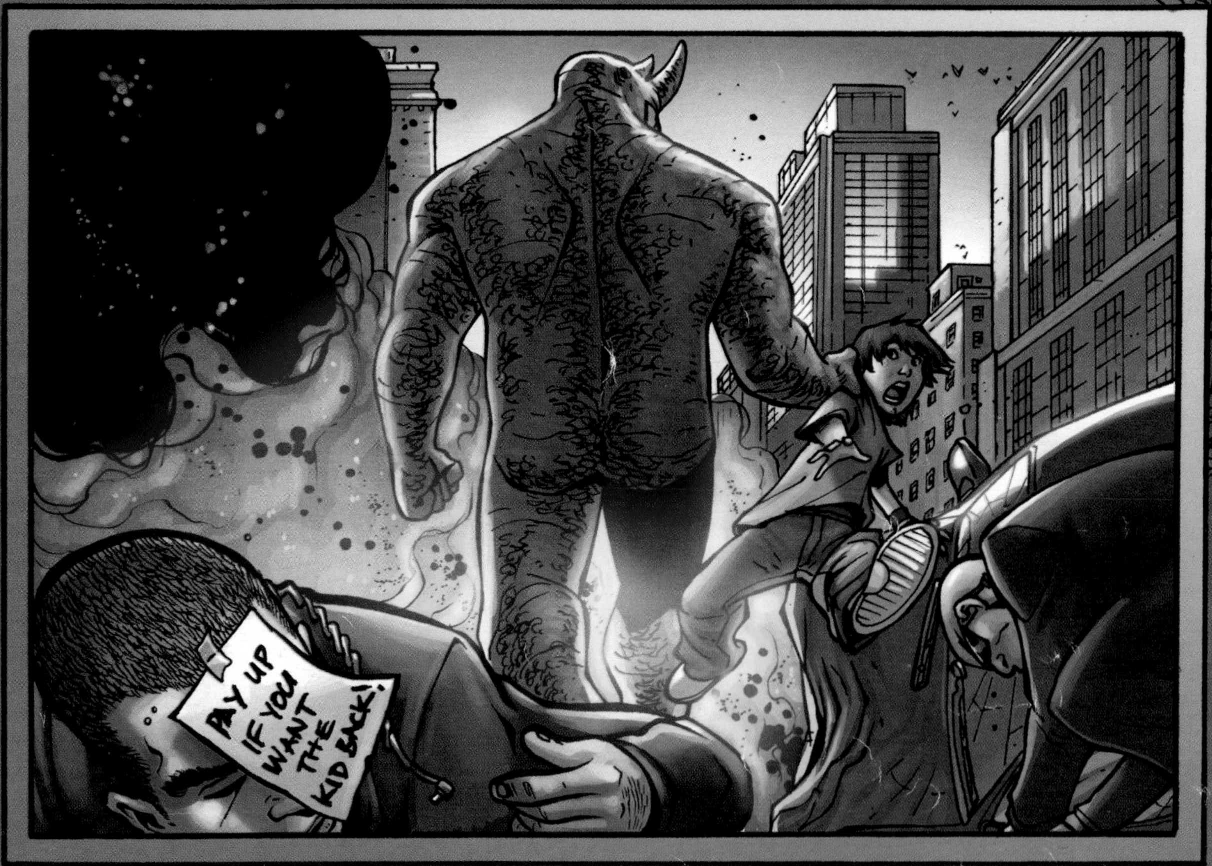
PAY UP IF YOU WANT THE KID BACK!

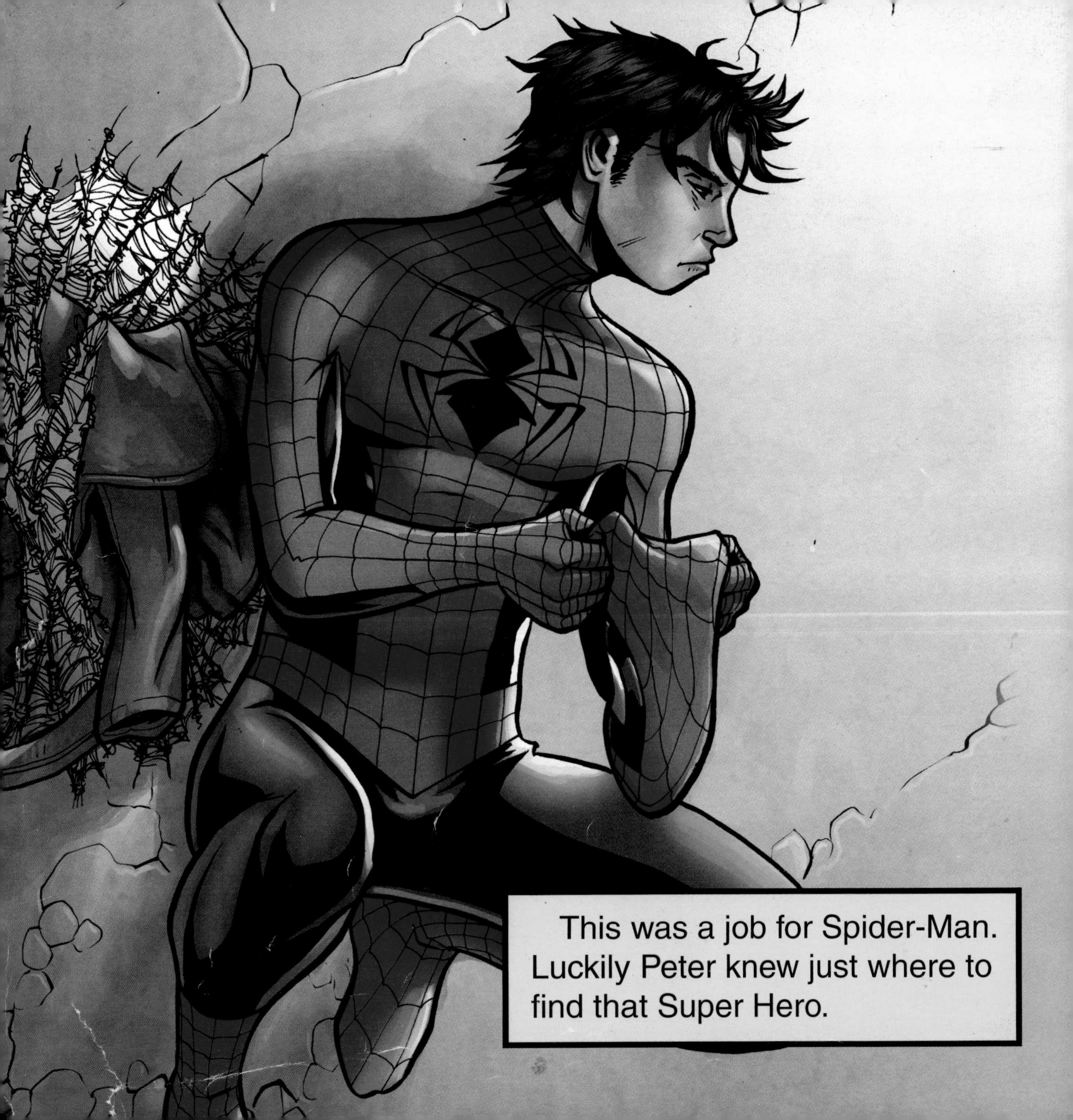

This was a job for Spider-Man. Luckily Peter knew just where to find that Super Hero.

Spider-Man swung from one part of the city to the next, hunting for the Rhino. As he came near an old warehouse, his spider-sense kicked in.

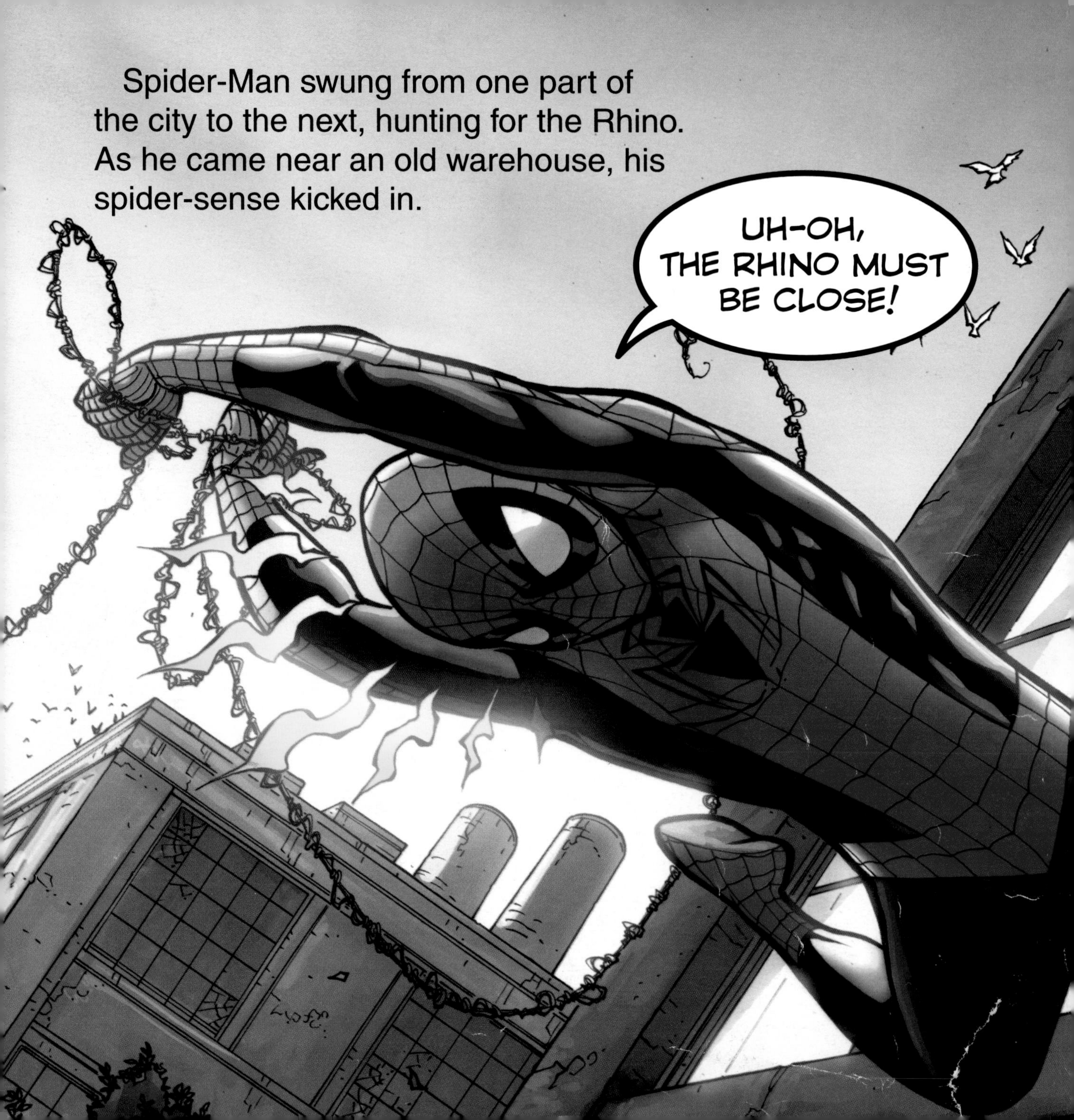
UH-OH, THE RHINO MUST BE CLOSE!

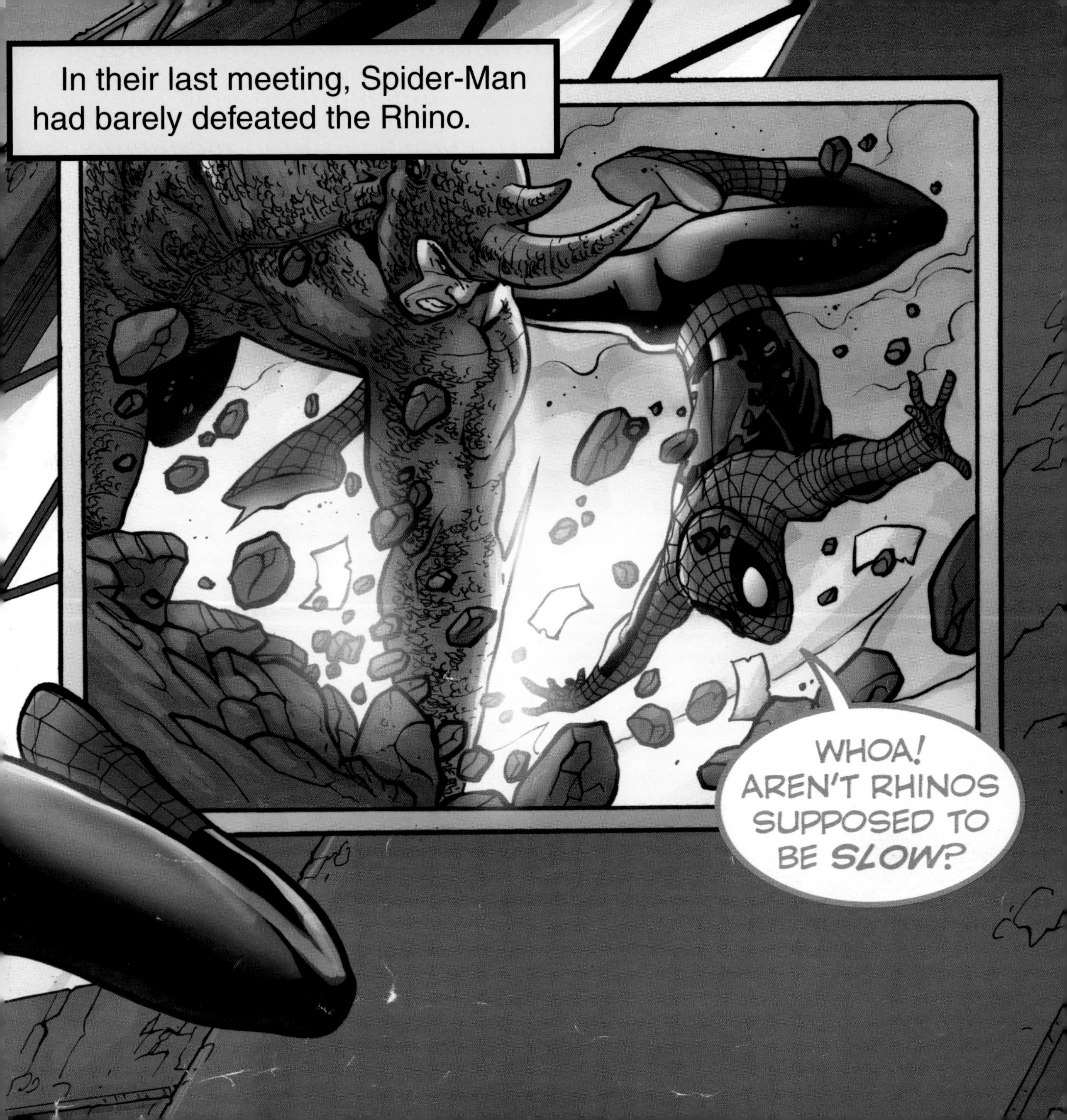
In their last meeting, Spider-Man had barely defeated the Rhino.
WHOA! AREN'T RHINOS SUPPOSED TO BE SLOW?

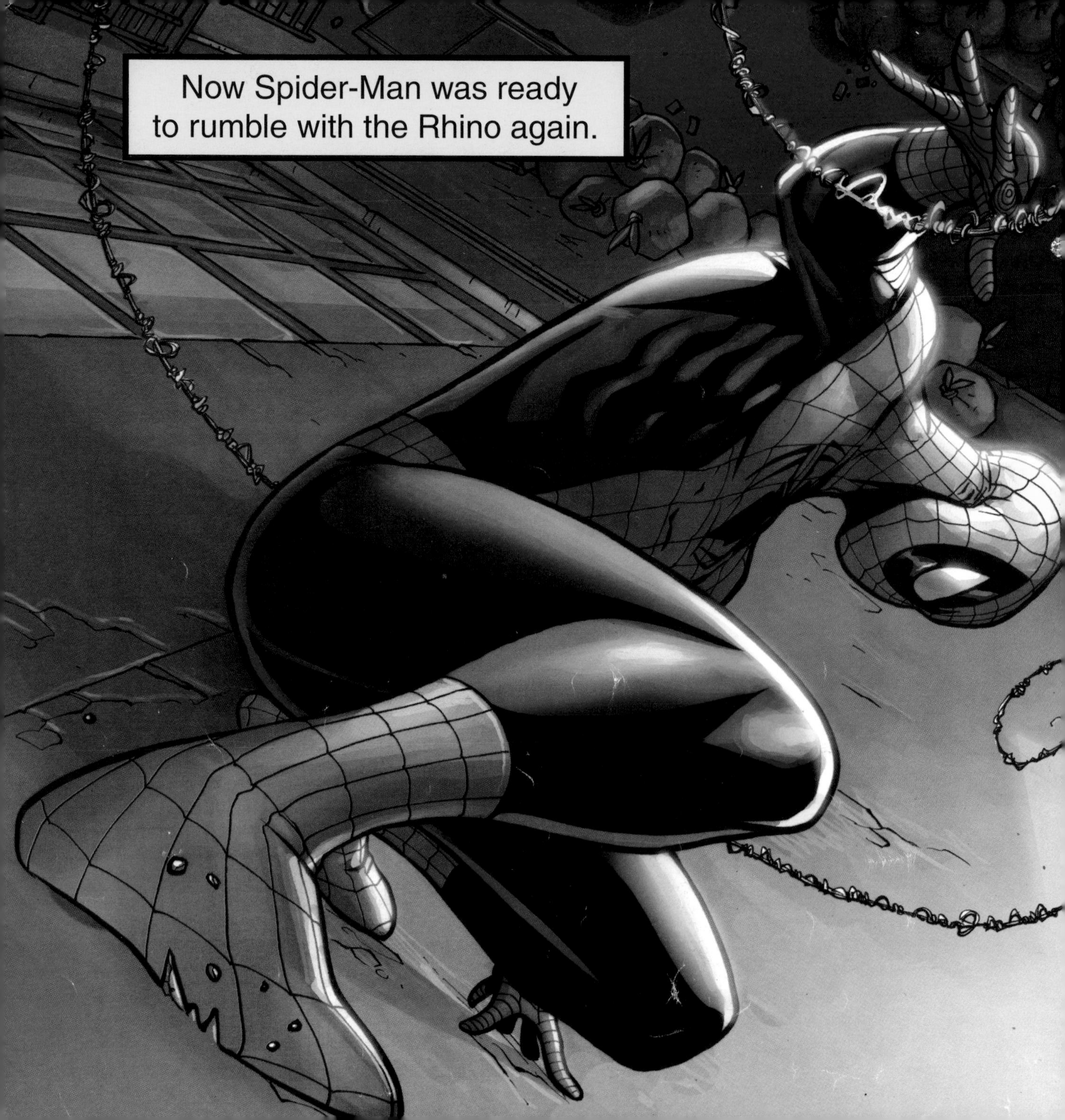
Now Spider-Man was ready to rumble with the Rhino again.

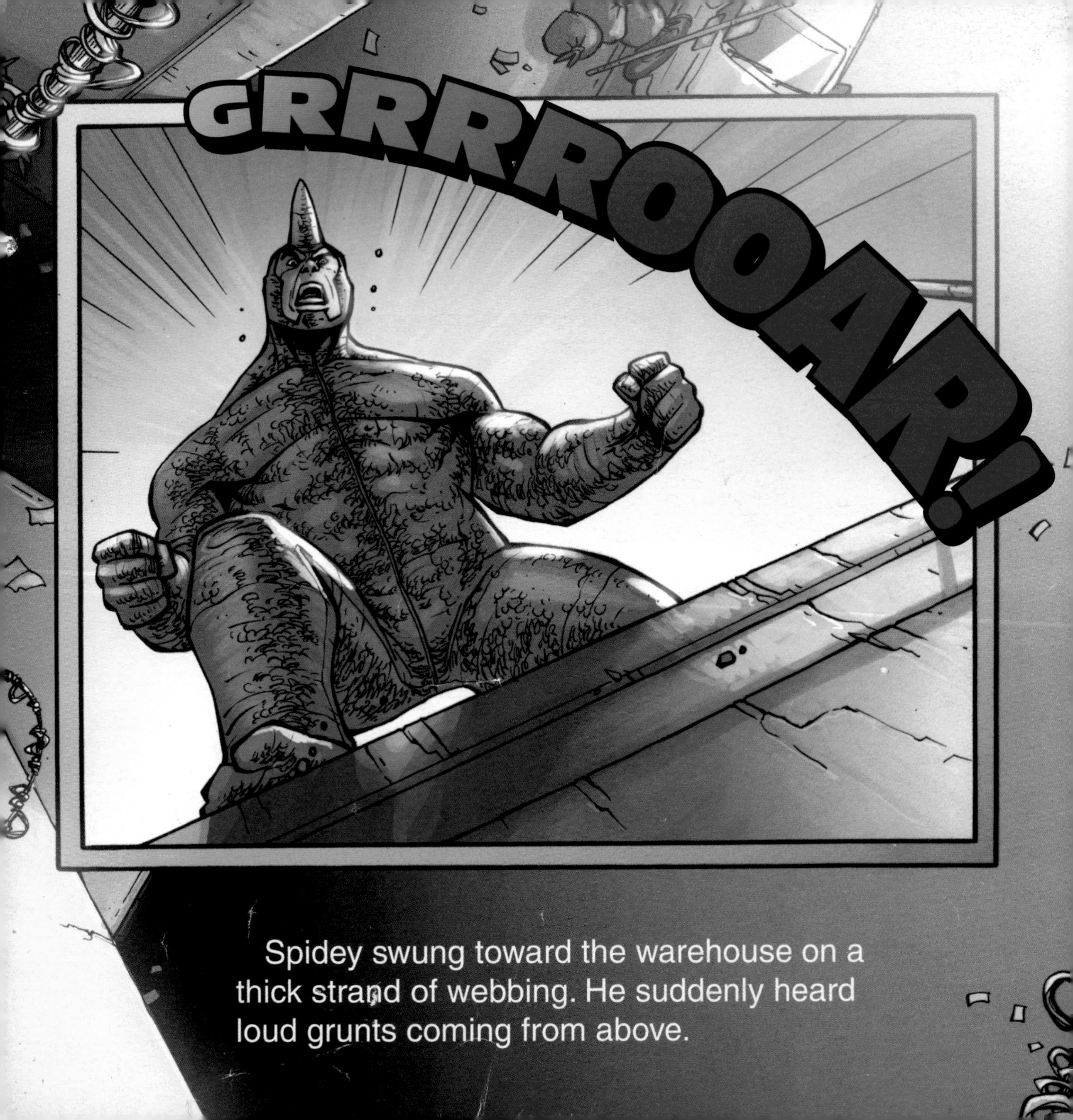
GRRRROOOAR!

Spidey swung toward the warehouse on a thick strand of webbing. He suddenly heard loud grunts coming from above.

That's a lot of rhino! Spider-Man thought as he pulled himself onto the roof.

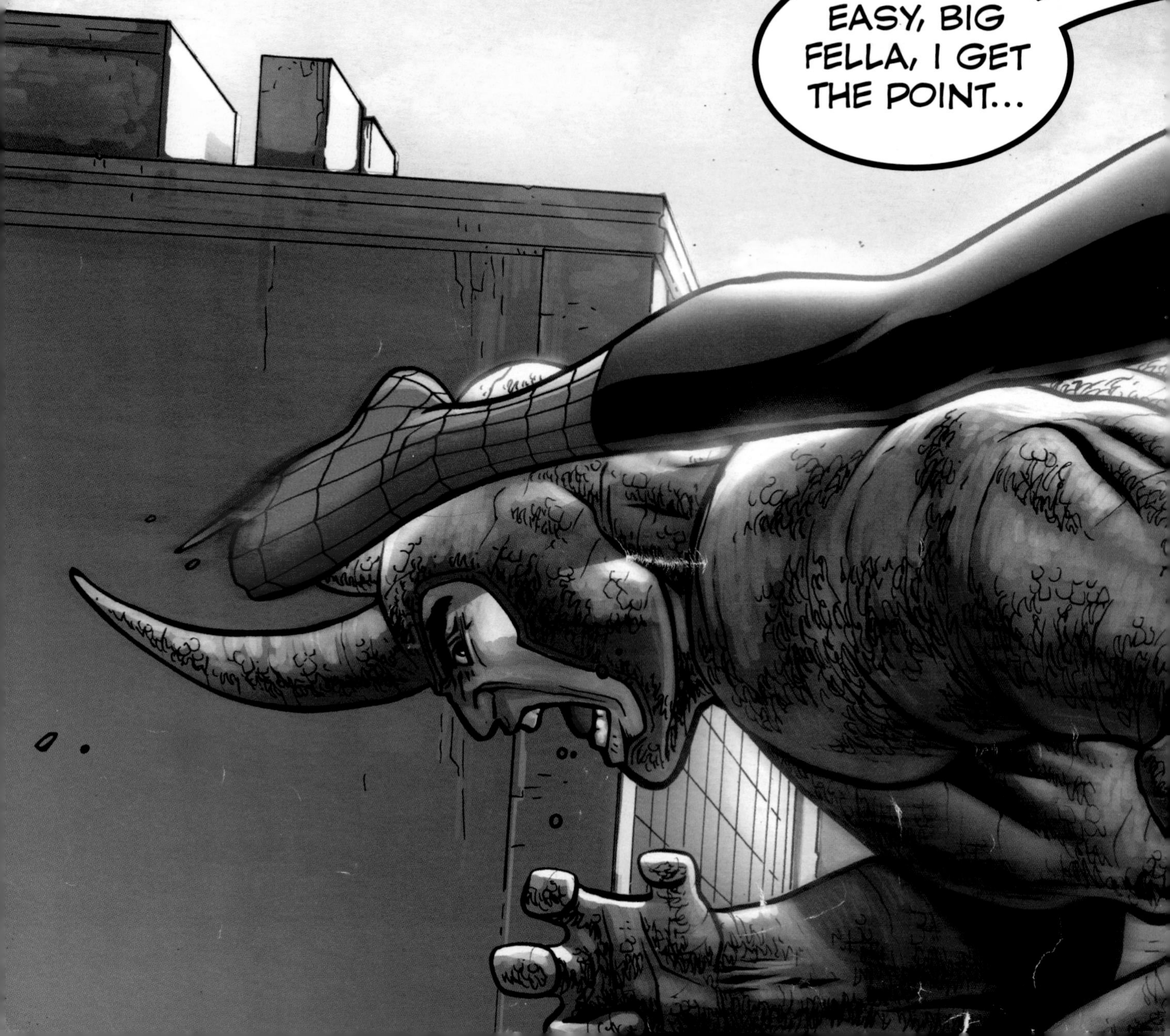
EASY, BIG FELLA, I GET THE POINT...

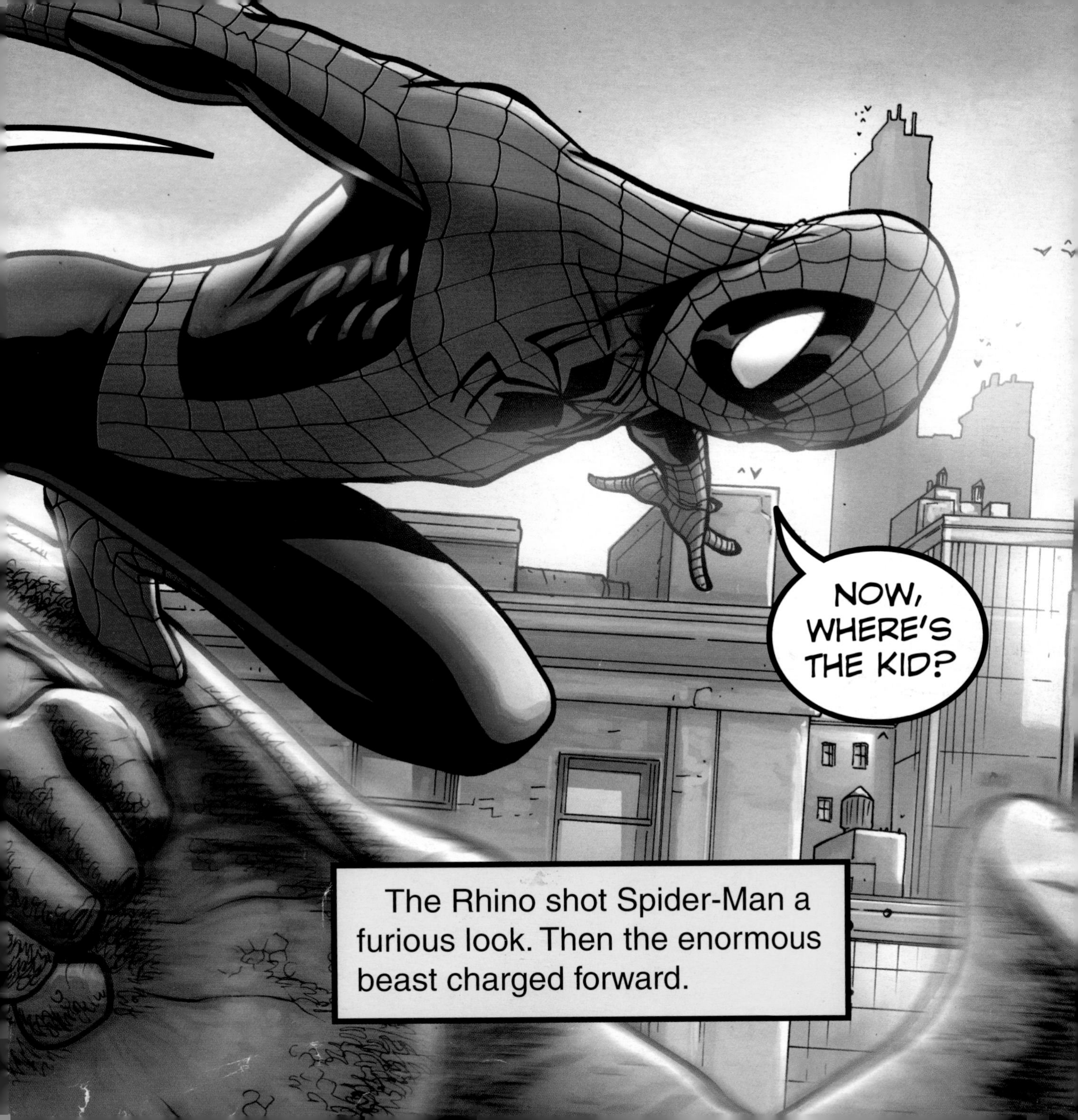
NOW, WHERE'S THE KID?
The Rhino shot Spider-Man a furious look. Then the enormous beast charged forward.

Spider-Man recovered quickly and jumped onto a nearby fire escape. Suddenly his spider-sense tingled. *The kid is definitely in there,* Spidey thought. He whisked through a window and into the dirty warehouse.

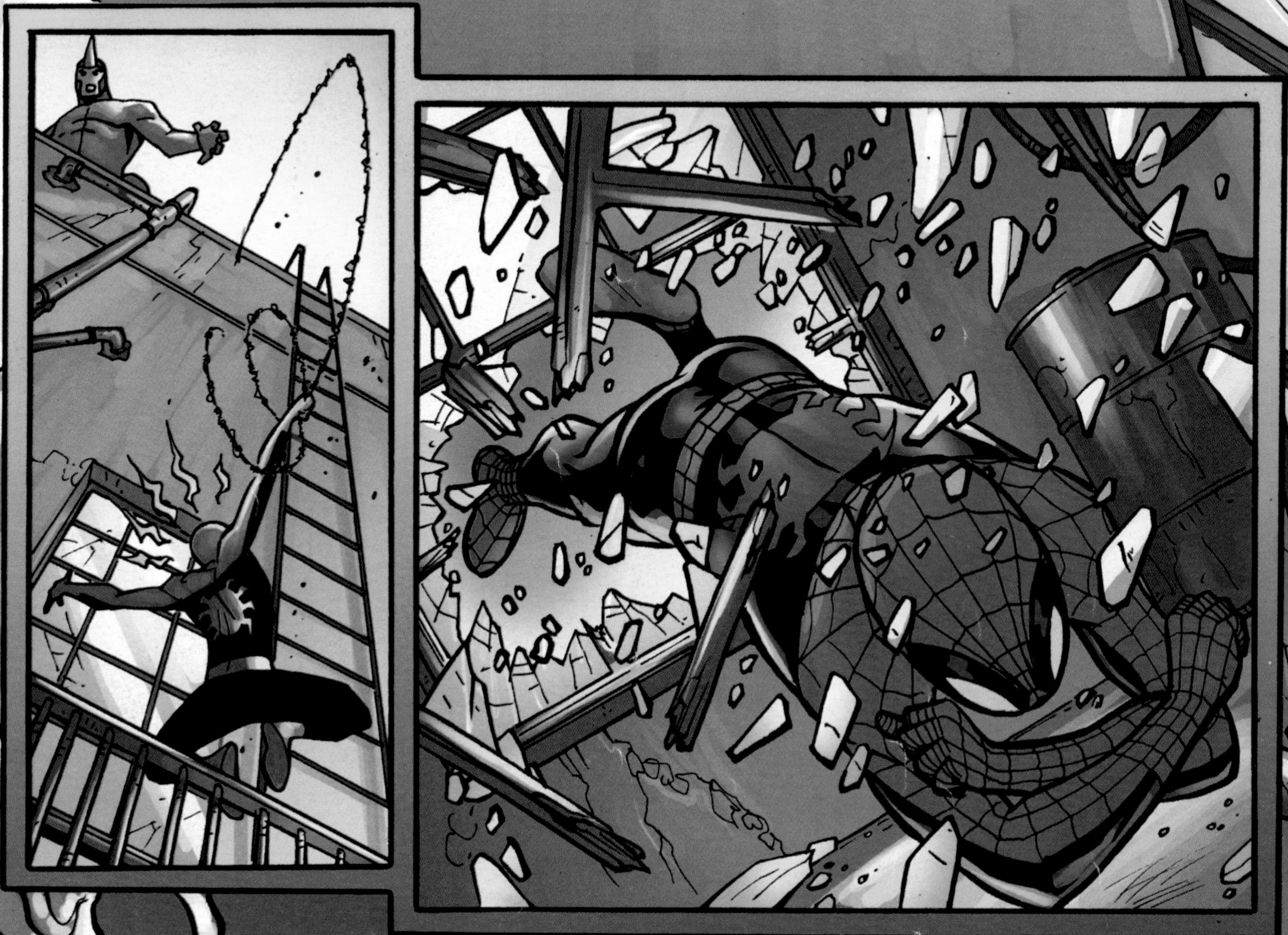

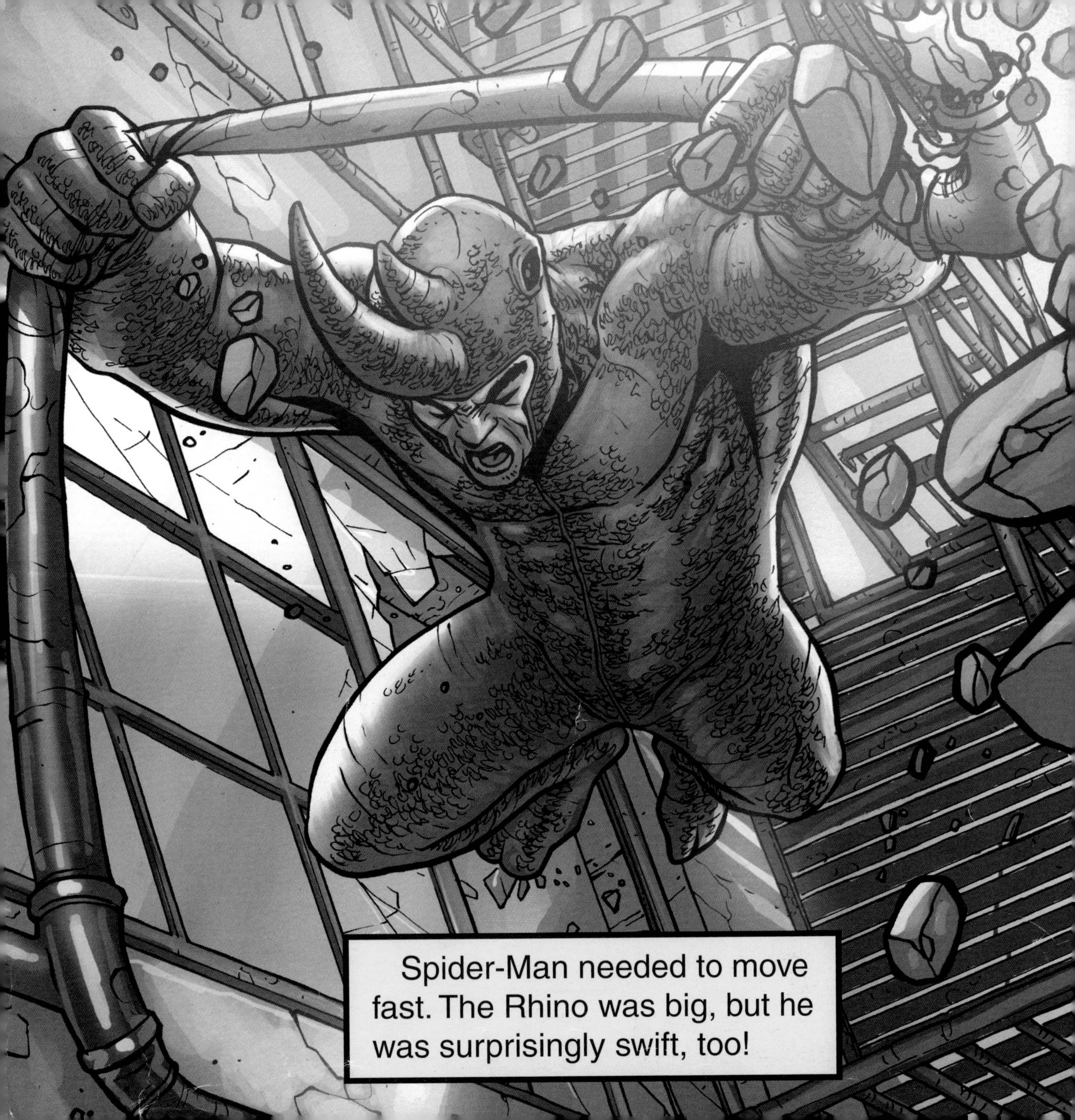

Spider-Man needed to move fast. The Rhino was big, but he was surprisingly swift, too!

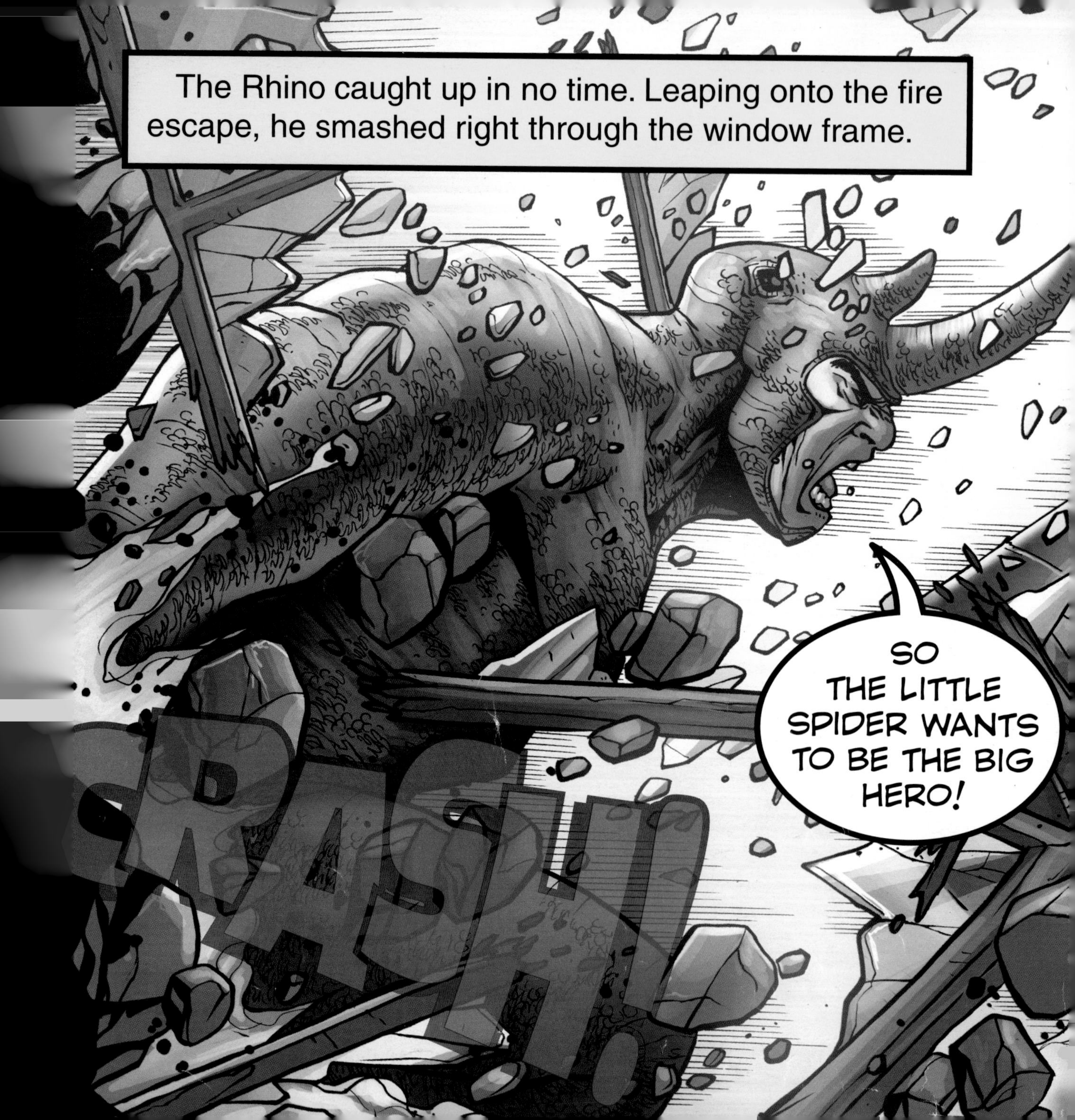
The Rhino caught up in no time. Leaping onto the fire escape, he smashed right through the window frame.
SO THE LITTLE SPIDER WANTS TO BE THE BIG HERO!
CRASH!

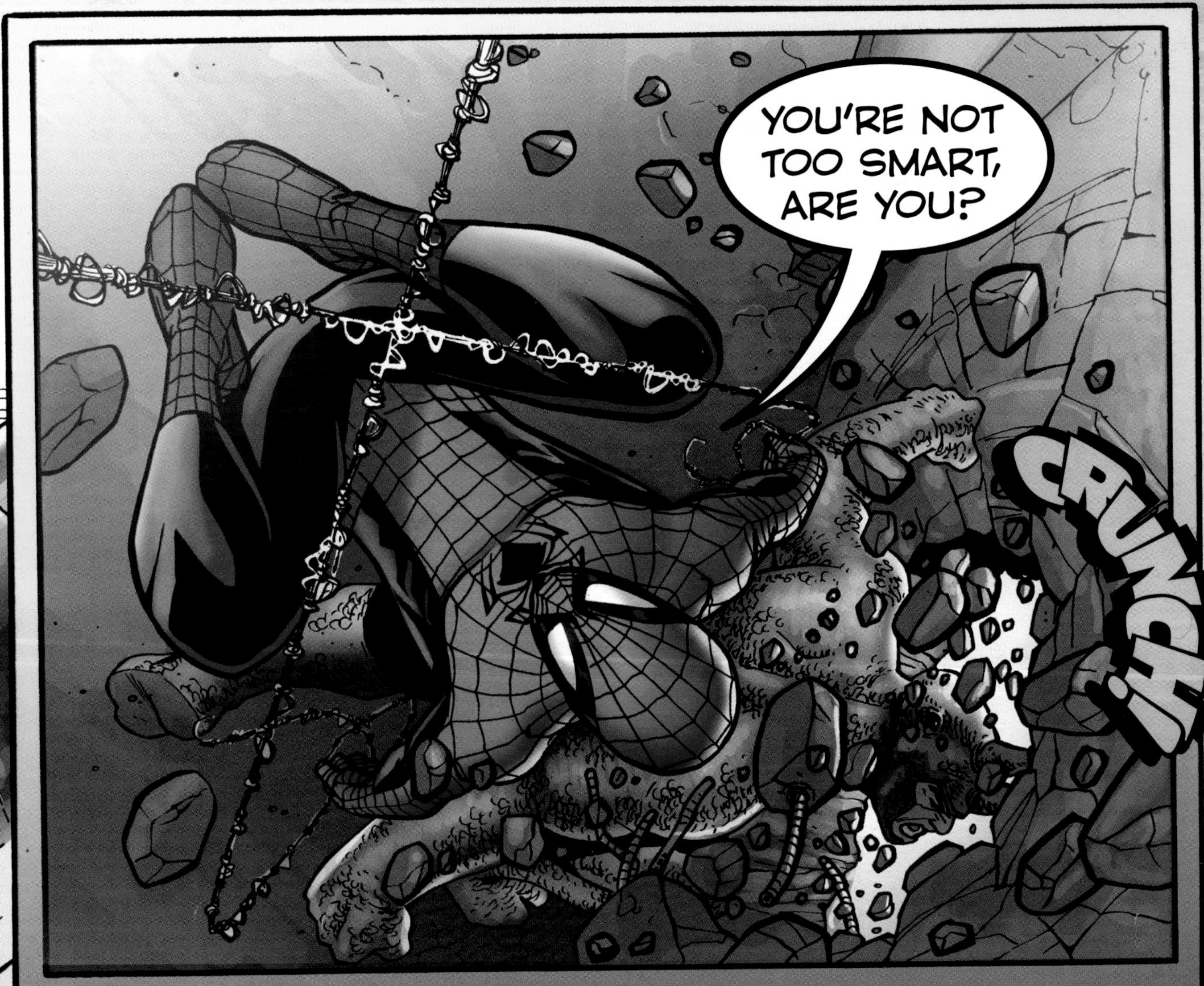
YOU'RE NOT TOO SMART, ARE YOU?
CRUNCH!

He charged Spider-Man at full speed. Spidey swung up toward the ceiling.

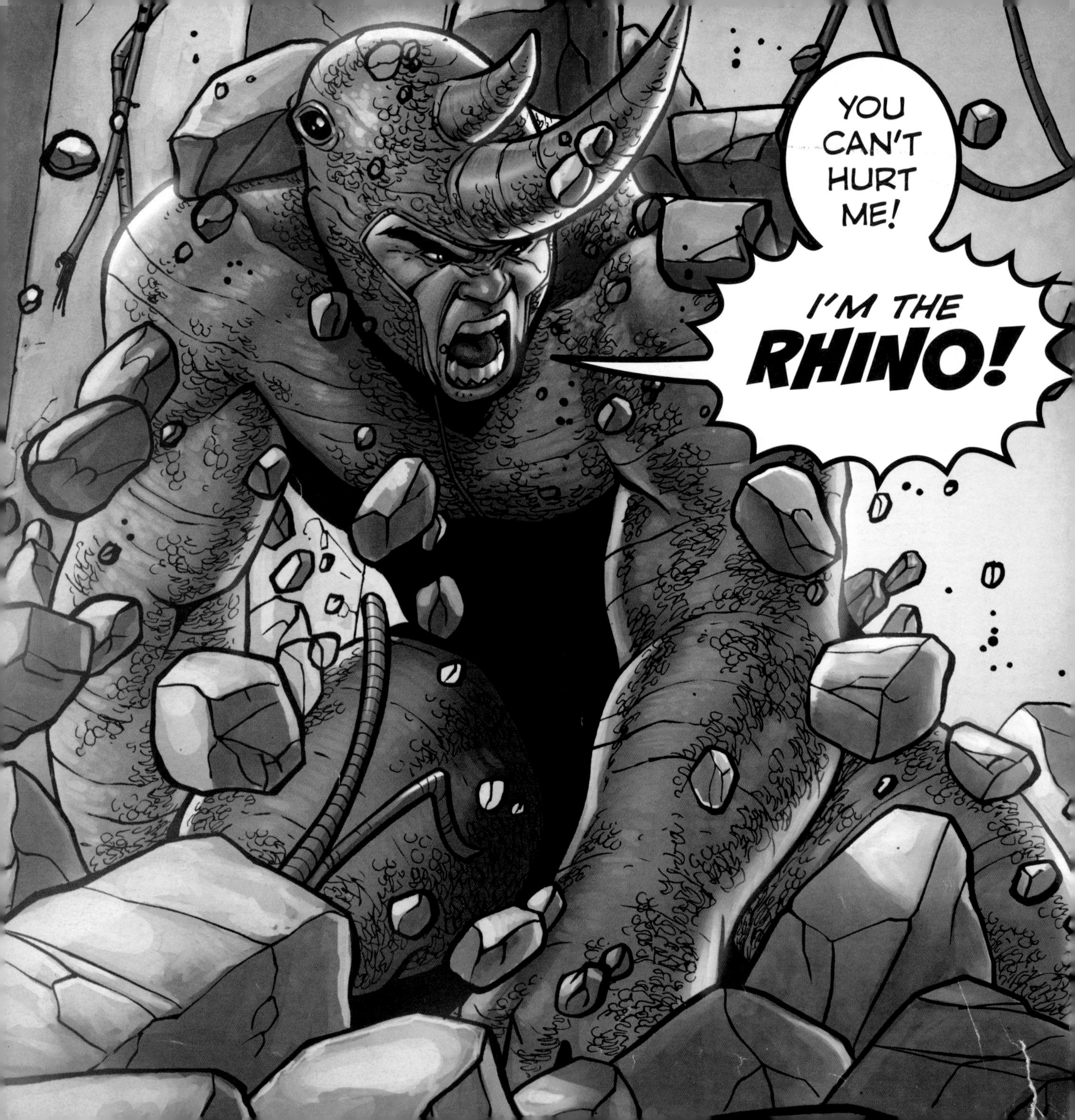
YOU CAN'T HURT ME!
I'M THE RHINO!

The Rhino pulled his gigantic body out from beneath the pile of bricks. Spider-Man waited until his enemy was back on his feet before making his move.

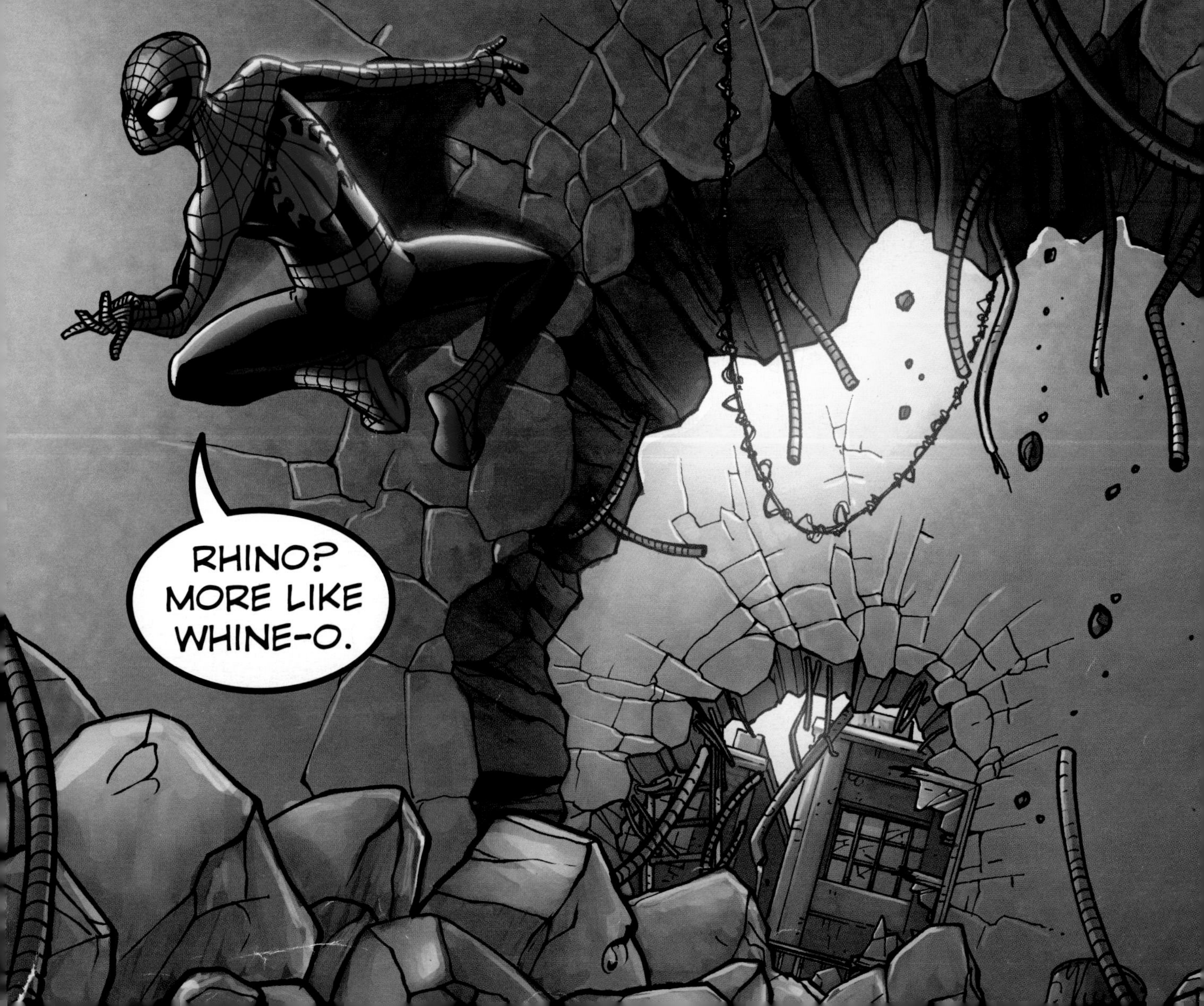
RHINO? MORE LIKE WHINE-O.

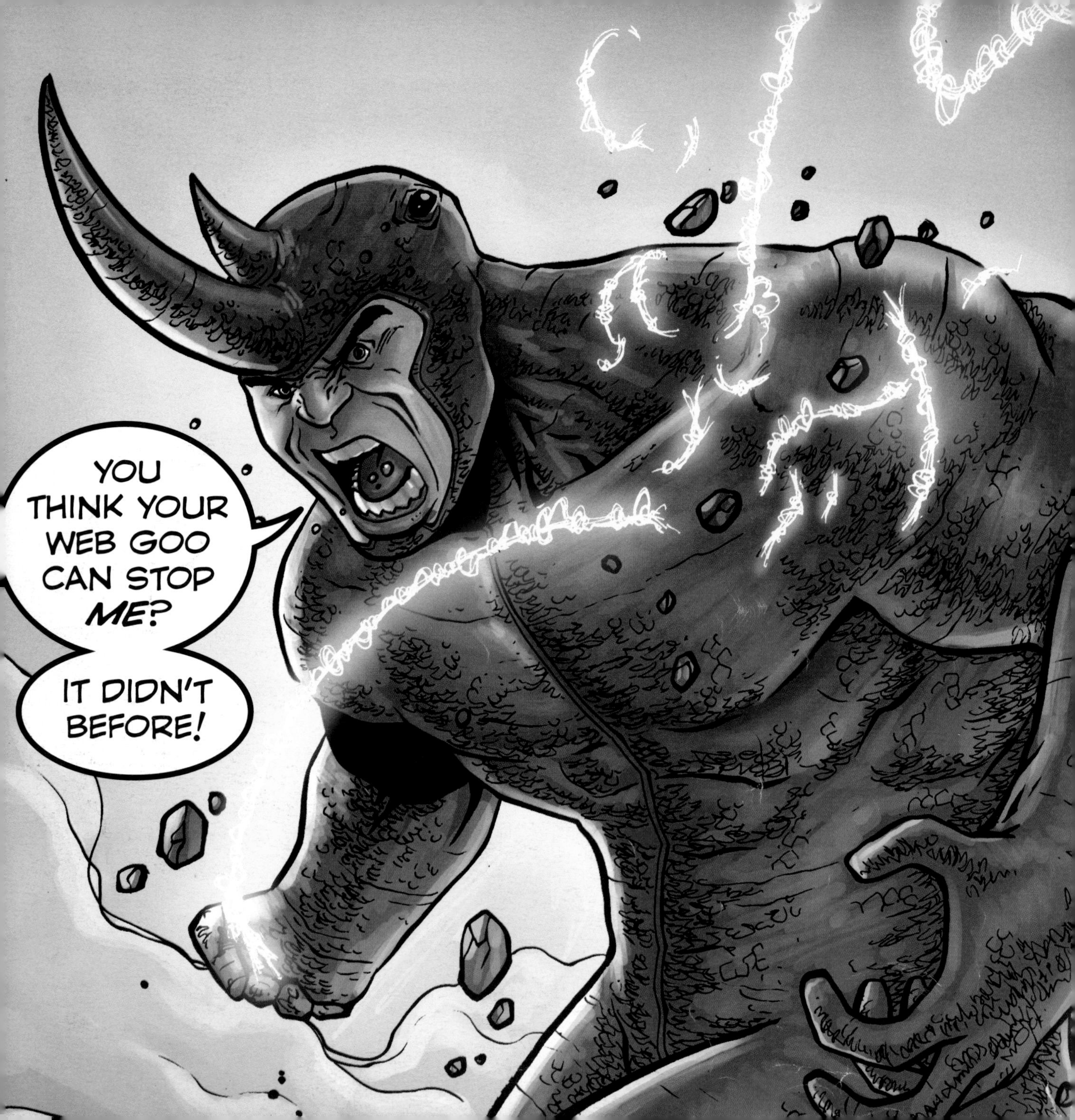
YOU THINK YOUR WEB GOO CAN STOP *ME*?
IT DIDN'T BEFORE!

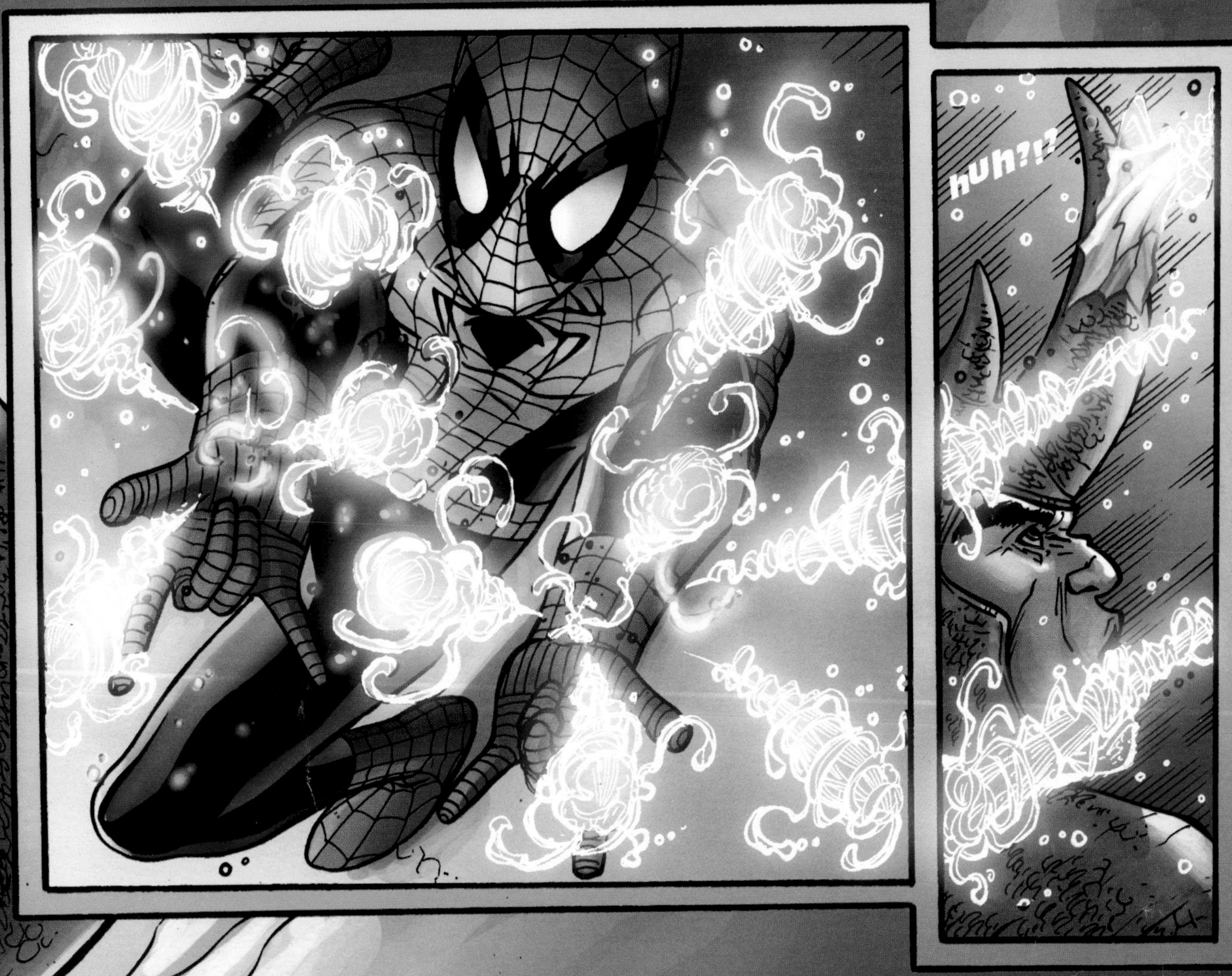
hUh?!?

But Spider-Man was prepared. Earlier he had loaded both of his shooters with a special web fluid that could freeze anything.

Spidey fired a stream of webbing that instantly stopped the Rhino in his tracks.

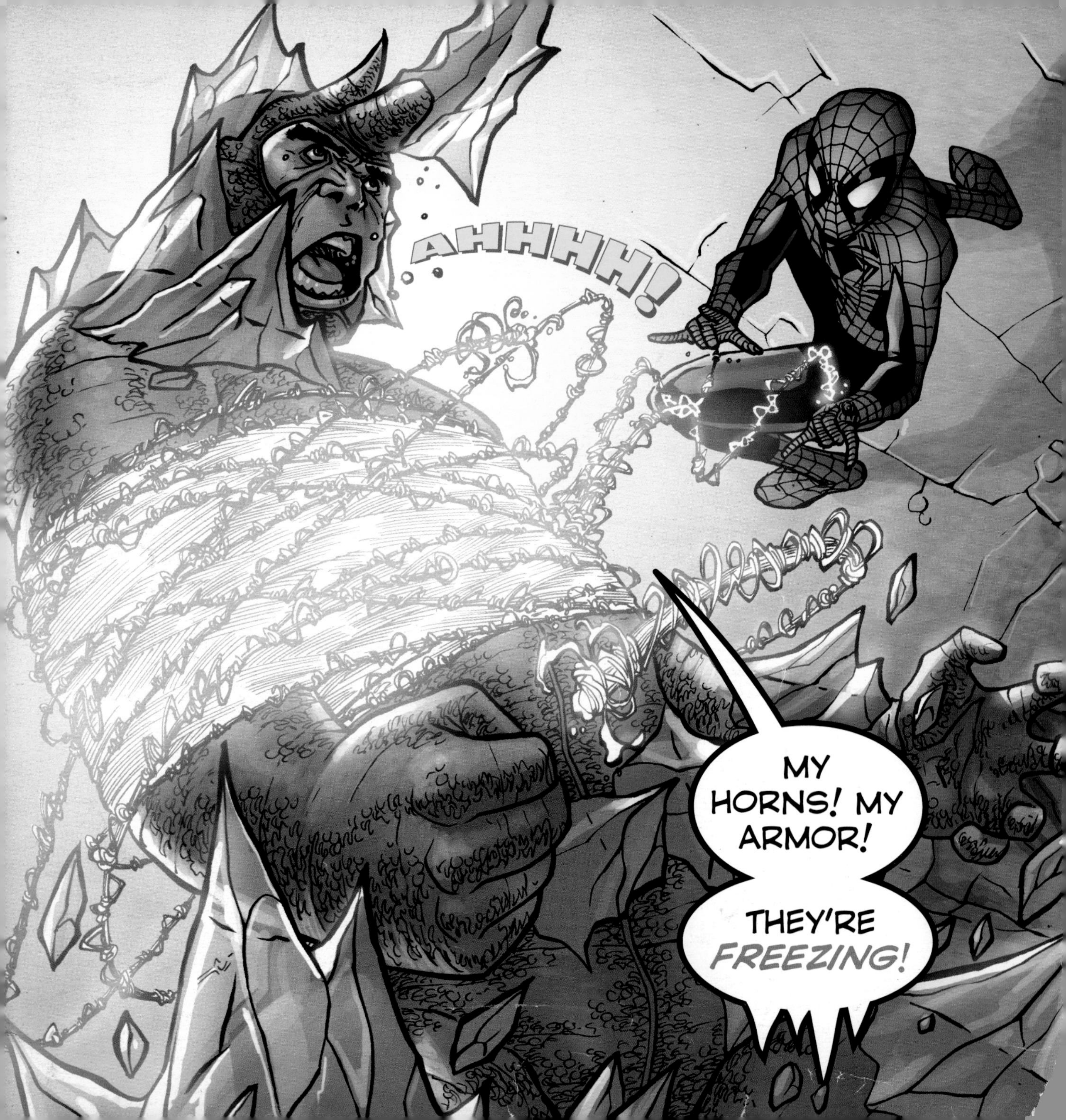
AHHHH!
MY HORNS! MY ARMOR!
THEY'RE FREEZING!

The Rhino stood completely still.
Spider-Man easily wrapped him in layers of web silk.
He reached for his camera.

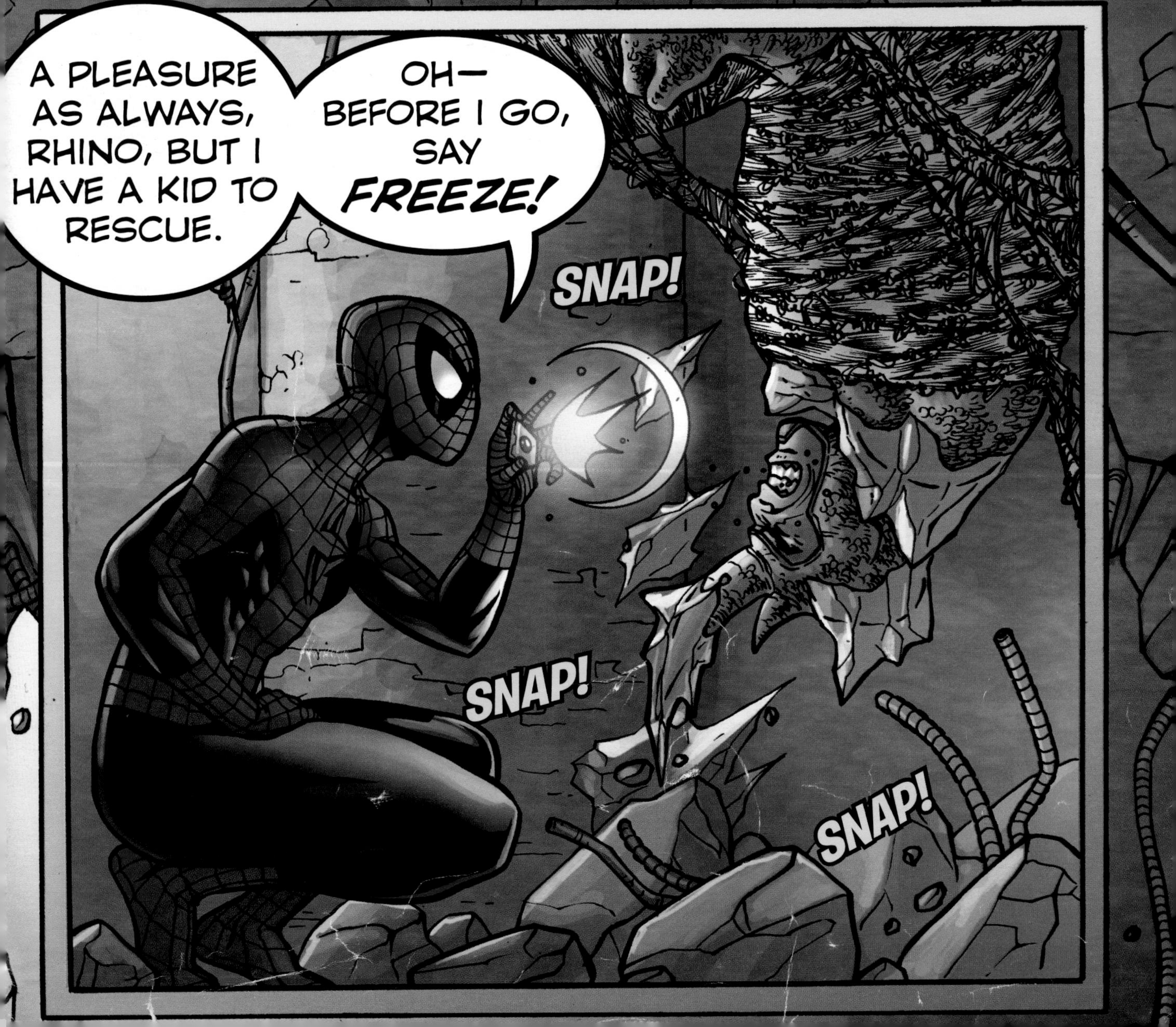
A PLEASURE AS ALWAYS, RHINO, BUT I HAVE A KID TO RESCUE.
OH— BEFORE I GO, SAY *FREEZE!*
SNAP!
SNAP!
SNAP!

Peter Parker handed in great photos of the Rhino. But Jameson barked, "Today's news is old news! I need new pictures, Parker!"

Peter Parker just could not win.

But at that moment, not even Jameson could ruin Peter's mood.

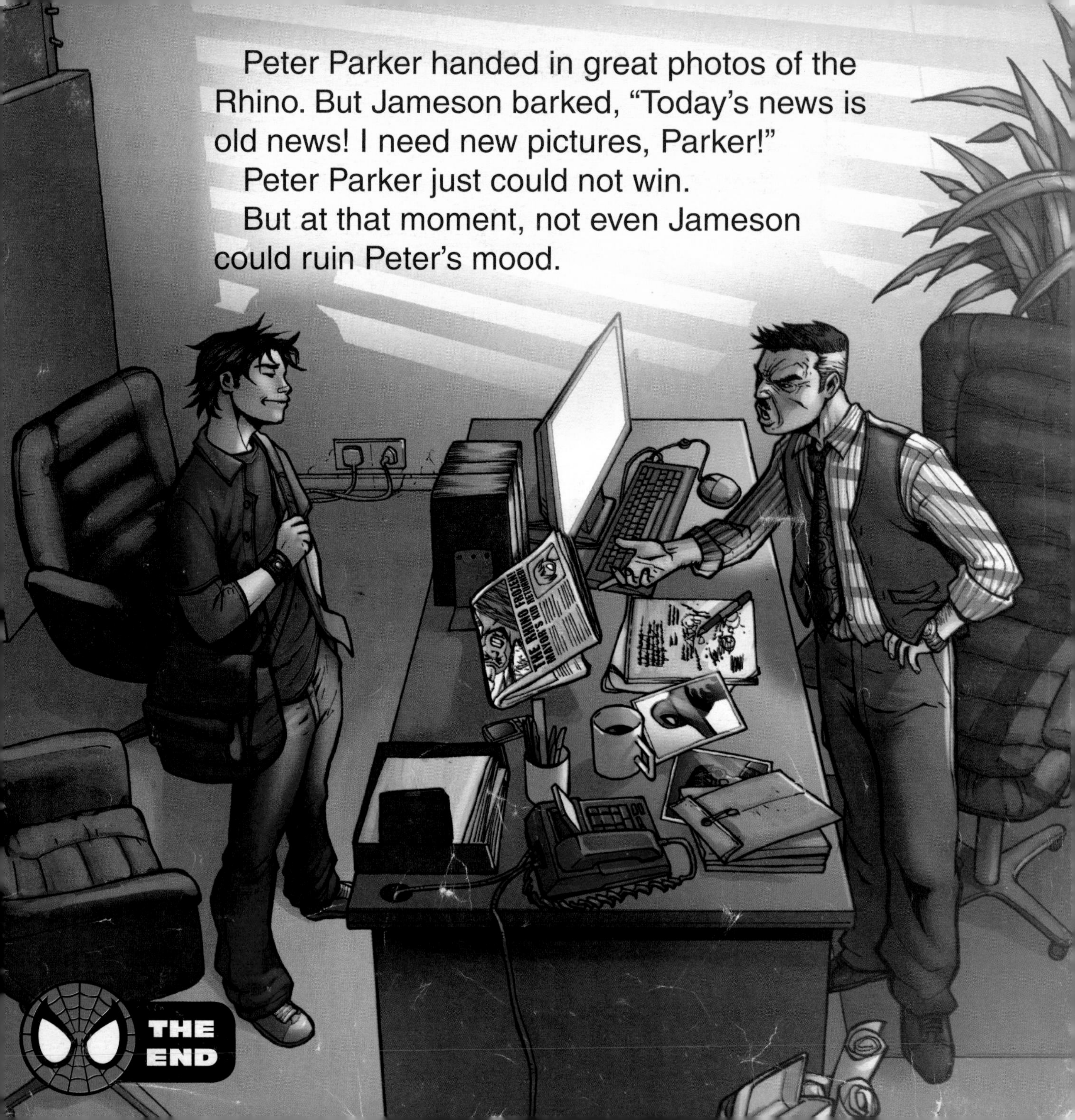
THE RHINO FROZEN!
MAYOR'S KID RETURNED!
THE END